# A Laugh in the Dark

# A
# LAUGH IN THE DARK

## AND OTHER
## MINNESOTA STATE PARK
## GHOST STORIES

Gary W. Fehring

NORTH STAR PRESS OF ST. CLOUD, INC.
St. Cloud, Minnesota

Illustrations by: Charles Fehring

ISBN-10: 0-87839-382-X
ISBN-13: 978-0-87839-382-4

First Edition, September 1, 2010

Printed in the United States of America

Published by
North Star Press of St. Cloud, Inc.
P.O. Box 451
St. Cloud, Minnesota 56302

www.northstarpress.com

# Table of Contents

This collection is dedicated to the seventy-two, soon to be seventy-three, Minnesota State Parks and all the great things to be experienced in these gifts of nature. It would be a grave injustice should anything in the stories lead to a sense of apprehension about paying these fine places a visit. To forestall any such thing taking place, please keep in mind the truth so well expressed by the crew of *Veggie Tales*. Remember that, "God is greater than the boogieman."

Gary

# THE ARMS OF ORVILLE VINCENTI

## A GREAT RIVER BLUFFS STATE PARK GHOST STORY

I F YOU HAPPEN TO VISIT Great River Bluffs State Park in southeastern Minnesota, there are a few things you should know about a man you might meet there. His name is Orville Theodore Vincenti. The first thing you want to do is be aware that Orville is mean as hell. Then if you are planning to camp at the park, you better know that Orville isn't going to like you. The man has an intense hatred of people who camp, especially at this particular park. Know that Orville has long arms, really long arms. It's also kind of important to understand that Orville Theodore Vincenti is dead, has been for quite a while now.

Orville grew up mean. He inherited his meanness from his dad, Alphonse Vincenti. The first time his dad hit him was when Orville was three days old and his crying woke the old man up. From then on inflicting injury on his son became, along with his abuse of alcohol, a part of the elder Vincenti's daily routine.

Introducing grievous bodily injury into other people's lives was how Alphonse Vincenti paid the rent on the family's southside Chicago apartment. Alphonse belonged to an association of immigrants that expected the community in which they resided to fund their lifestyle by giving them money Alphonse and his associates would otherwise have to earn by gainful employment. When one or another of their neighbors objected to that arrangement Alphonse was sent out to see if a month or two in traction might improve their attitude.

It was his father's unfortunate habit of bringing his work home that instilled in the growing boy a well spring of hostility, which he carried with him throughout his time on earth, both being alive and not.

Before his father's demise, when some men with guns called him to account for his behavior in the northside garage on the previous Valentine's Day, Little Al, as the association had come to recognize him, introduced Orville to Big Al. Seeing in the young man a disregard for the value of human life even greater than his own, Big Al opened a spot in the organization that Orville, after dissuading his competitors by creating a collection of widows and orphans, fit himself into.

The extraordinary length of Orville Theodore's arms was noted first by the midwife who delivered him. Looking at the infant, the good woman puzzled over how such a thing could be. The distance between the family's residence and Chicago's two zoological gardens seemed to preclude any of their inhabitants being a factor in the newborn's physical appearance. Having a compassionate nature of a kind unshared by anyone else in the apartment, including the Vincenti family's newest member, she refrained from commenting either publicly or privately on the boy's resemblance to certain creatures of the jungle which spent the greater part of their lives swinging in the trees.

It was not compassion but fear that prompted the woman's fellow human beings to follow her example. At first it was fear of Alphonse's reaction to anything negative being suggested about the fruit of his loins. Later it was fear of Orville himself.

Even Big Al, who privately referred to his employee as Orville the Orangoutan, never had the courage to indulge in such witticism in Orville's presence.

Because Orville's companions were so intimidated by the unlimited hostility storming in what would be a soul in other people, and because their bladders had the unpleasant practice of releasing their contents should Orville unexpectedly show up among them, these otherwise fearless enemies of law and order issued a passionate request to the boss for the removal of Orville to someplace where even his memory would disappear in the distance. Siberia was suggested.

Big Al was not convinced that the government in that part of the world, as murderous was it was showing itself to be, would accept a presence as malignant as Orville in their territory. Instead he did what he considered to be the next best thing and deported Orville to rural Minnesota to be the caretaker of the organization's property along Highway 61 between LaCrosse, Wisconsin, and Winona, Minesota

Used by those engaged in criminal activity as a private rest area between Big Al's Chicago and the sanctuary provide by the city police in St. Paul, the lodge at the foot of the bluffs was felt to be as safe a place to locate Orville Theodore Vincenti as could be found this side of the grave. An added bonus was that Orville could reach most of what needed tending without having to use a ladder.

Although taking refuge in wooded areas was common practice among the Midwest's criminal element, not all of those who did so could be considered nature lovers. Those who were, and who happened to spend some time at the lodge, were horrified by what they encountered there. Not only was the place absolutely unkempt in the care of the southside Chicago ape man, but, unlike many others in the animal kingdom, he tended to provide very little distance between where he ate and where he performed certain other bodily functions. Furthermore, the grounds were littered with the bodies of woodland creatures who happened to wander into his enormous reach.

Unable to expend his hostility onto his fellow humans, Orville took it out on whatever else around him lived and breathed. The lodge, it turned out, had not been the best place to have put him. Six feet under would have been better.

Big Al's decision to do that, or at least render Orville into a physical condition that a concern for public health would recommend such an internment, was not reached because of *who* Orville was, but because of *what* Orville said.

Orville, unlike so many guests of Great River Bluffs State Park, had never stuck his head, or any other part of his anatomy, inside a tent. The man was not a happy camper. The beauty and pristine purity of his surroundings at the lodge offended his sense of life's ugliness and degradation. He missed seeing the filth of Chicago at it's worst. He missed hearing the sound of gunfire, fists striking flesh, the whimpers of those he regarded as annoying, and the sirens of the ambulances coming to collect what was left of them.

Overwhelmed by the unfairness of his situation, Orville drank too much. Worst still for his health, Orville talked to much. When a lodge visitor reported to Big Al the comment an inebriated Orville made about an impropriety in Al's relationship with his mom, the boss sent a car full of his associates to solve, once and for all, the Orville problem.

Among those packed into the Packard sedan was a man whose avocation singled him out from the others. The guy actually liked walking in the woods without bringing with him some poor slob who wouldn't be walking out. During the time he had spent in the lodge he had climbed the bluff overlooking the property and remembered there being a primitive campground near the edge and a road leading to it from the west. He suggested the group try their hand at camping. For recreation they could bring Orville, bound securely, to the top of the bluff and push him off.

Instilling in his companions a spirit of adventure unknown to them since their youth, the group stopped in LaCrosse to outfit themselves with the required equipment. After locating the farm road leading to the bluff, they followed it to its end and set up camp. That completed the quartet of killers returned to the highway and made their way to the lodge.

The place was a wreck. As much as the Chicago boys disliked sleeping in tents, they were glad that they had alternative sleeping accommodations away from the stinking shambles Orville's caretaking had made of the association's property.

Using a medication provided to them by a compliant Chicago pharmacist the group had no problem rendering Orville amenable to being wrapped in several layers of good stout hemp. One doctored drink had done the job.

It wasn't easy to haul the inert Orville to the auto and horse him in, but, after the hard work of getting Ted the Tang to the bluff top campground, it was time for fun. First in the evening's entertainment was waking Orville up by taking turns urinating on his face. Following that, they built a campfire and sat around it, the bound Orville among them. The evening was spent singing long forgotten camp songs, regaling Orville with hilarious accounts of what they were going to do with him and what it would feel like to him when they did it.

None of what they said did anything more than increase Orville's hatred of human beings in general and camping and campers in particular. While his inner being busied itself with anger, his outer being busied itself with loosening the ropes which bound him.

Unlike what mobsters do in the movies, the boys from Chicago had little practice tying people up. Typically, they just shot people they didn't like.

On this occasion, had they been Boy Scouts working on a merit badge for knot tying, they would have flunked tho toot.

Making good use of his fingers and his handy opposable thumbs, Orville was able to work the ends of the rope around to where he could reach the knot and begin to loosen the clump any self-respecting sailor would have regarded with scorn. By the time the campers from Chicago finished their last song and consumed their last toasted marshmallow, Orville had nearly disunited the two ends of the rope his captors expected would hold him fast.

When the suggestion was made that it was time to turn in. The boys decided they had better do so before they got too drunk to find their tents. Getting up from the glowing coals of what had been their campfire Big Al's crew realized they had one last task to perform before crawling into the comfort of their army surplus sleeping bags.

Lifting Orville to his feet, they nudged him along to the edge of the bluff and pushed him over.

Things seemed to have gone well until the dimness of their inebriation receded enough for several of them to realize that when Ted the Tang was stepping off into the air he was leaving behind the rope which bound him. Extending his arms as he began his journey to the rocks below,

Orville gathered in the men pushing him and took them with him, all but one.

It's said there are people just too mean to die. If that's true, it certainly would have been true for Orville Theodore Vincenti. Orville was pretty mean, but, when his decent from the bluff was completed, he was also pretty dead. Then again, perhaps there is some truth in that saying, because Orville's meanness wasn't going to let him stay dead.

If that one guy hadn't been left behind when Orville dragged his associates off the bluff to spend a few final moments with him dancing in the air, the bluff overlooking the lodge would be a much safer place to visit. As it is Orville, mean and angry, can't get that failure out of his ghostly system. He's never stopped being after the man missed by his open arms

You've been warned. Should you choose to camp at the Great River Bluffs State Park in Minnesota, you need to remember that Orville Theodore Vincenti isn't going to like you. If he can't get his hands on the guy who helped push him off the bluff, he'd just as soon get his hands on someone . . . maybe you.

The views from the bluffs in that park are outstanding. There are times walking the trails when the sparkling beauty of the Mississippi River can take your breath away. Orville the Orangoutan is ready to do that, too. I can't tell you just how far away from the edge of the bluff you need to stay to be out of Orville's reach. All I can tell you is that Orville, alive and dead, has long arms, really long arms.

# THE BEAR RIDER

## A SPLIT ROCK LIGHTHOUSE GHOST STORY

MY NAME IS DEREK PIKE, and I am eleven years old. If I had lived another week, I would have been twelve. I looked forward to being twelve. When I was twelve, my father told me, I could help him tend the light.

How I love that light. I watch it still, shining atop our lighthouse high above the stormy lake people named Superior. My father was the lighthouse keeper. We lived there, my father and mother and my two sisters. My sisters were twins, six years older than I was when, a week before my birthday, I met the bear.

You may have been to our home. It is the one closest to the lighthouse. If you look carefully when you visit, you'll see some of the toys I left behind. My favorite is the lighthouse carved for me by the men who helped my father. It was their gift on the last Christmas my family and I spent together before that fateful day the bear came.

Where we lived, isolated on that great cliff, was, for my mother and my sisters, a lonely place.

It wasn't for me. In the summer, when my father was finished with his work, he took me fishing, sometimes in the lake, sometimes along the Bull Rock River. In the winter, on our skis or snowshoes, my father and I would go hunting. It was all so exciting.

During the summer when my father was at work and my lessons were over for the day, I explored the forest on my own. "Don't get lost," my mother told me, and off I would go.

Getting lost was the only danger to avoid. But, staying near the lake. I always knew where home was and how to get there. Of all the animals in the wilderness, even wolves and bear, except for one bear, none threatened me. Seeing me without my father and the powerful gun he carried with him, the woodland creatures seemed to regard me as a companion and a friend.

Beneath the great cliff into which our light and home were anchored there were the simple homes of some men who made their living fishing on the lake. My sisters were warned never to go there, and they never did. I did though. While I could not understand their language, Norwegian I was told, I enjoyed their boisterous company.

There was one man, whose name was Nels, who spoke English well enough so that if he spoke slowly, and I listened carefully, I could sort of undcrotand him. It was Nels who told me about the bear.

When the rock, which gave its name to the nearby river, was split, a spirit power was released. Seeking a body to inhabit, it found a bear cub lying alone and near death in a shallow cave beside the river. The cub's mother had been shot by the lighthouse keeper who had the job before our family came.

Infused by the spirit's power, the small cub not only survived the loss of its mother, but, growing to maturity, attained a size that dwarfed its forest cousins. Feeding only at night, and only when the roar of storm-driven waves pounding Superior's rocky shore masked the thunder of its movement through the forest, the great bear, ferocious and ageless, stalks its prey.

On those nights, Nels warned, when the wind blew hard and the great bear prowled to feed, stay at home and lock the doors. This warning, Nels said, was meant especially for my family and myself. While everyone was in danger from the great bear's hunger, the one it searched for above all others was the man who killed its mother—the lighthouse keeper—and, Nels continued, looking straight into my eyes, his hands on my shoulders, the lighthouse keeper's cubs. That, he said with caution, was . . . me.

Being frightened was not a new experience for me, but the story Nels related, and something about the way he looked and sounded when he told it, opened a depth of terror in my soul that rose up within me like a flood and propelled me up the cliffside to the safety of our home without my feet touching the ground a single time.

For the remainder of that day, my fear was such a force within me that I could not eat. That night I could not sleep. I lay in my bed, staring at the ceiling and seeing the looming figure of an angry bear in each moonlit shadow cast by the breeze blown movement of the window's curtain. They say there is such a thing as dying of fright. That is not true. If it were I would not have survived that long and awful night.

I DID SURVIVE. In the morning I found my father in his office and repeated the story told to me. His response to the tale that had caused me such alarm filled me with shame. He laughed out loud and shook his head at me as though I were a witless simpleton for giving any credit to such a foolish narrative. There was no such thing as a ghost bear. The Norwegian fisherman were as well known for the stories they told as for the fish they caught. "They must be chuckling still," he added, "at your falling for such nonsense."

"You should know better," my father told me. "Stories like that might frighten your mother and sisters, they being impressionable women, but we men," he said, "are made of sterner stuff." With that he ordered me to leave so that he might attend to important business.

I left my father's office with tear-filled eyes. I was both ashamed and angry. My anger was more with myself than with Nels and his companions. I had lost the most precious thing I had, my father's good opinion of his son.

I WAS GOING TO SHOW my father the kind of man I was, even at eleven. The next night when the wind blew across the lake and all sound was lost save for the roaring of the white-capped waves, I went, alone, into the forest.

Knowing my parents would stop me if they knew what I intended, I waited until the family was asleep. Then I dressed and left. Careful to avoid being seen by the attendant who minded the light and horn, I hid in the shadows when the lighthouse beam passed over me. As it passed, I charted my path and followed it in the dark until I crossed the clearing and was among the trees.

I would not go far, but I would go. When I returned, I would tell my father what I had done and take note of his pride when he understood the kind of man he had fathered in his little son. I would not be swayed by an old man's stories.

I was frightened though. Although the forest had been home to me, that night I felt like a stranger. I was were I had no business being, on a night when I had no business being out. How much time it would take to prove my manhood, I did not know. Not long, I hoped. I turned toward the lake and the light. In the light beam as it struck the woods, I saw the bear, the huge and hungry bear.

Now, I RIDE THAT BEAR. The Split Rock spirit which has given this animal its endless life has brought the same to me, and made me the great bear's spirit guide. The murder of its mother had been avenged when the bear brought me to death. While the spirit bear no longer stalks the lighthouse people, it still prowls the woods on those nights the wind blows across the lake. I have satisfied its anger, but not its hunger.

Listen to me carefully. When the storm stirs up Superior's water and its waves pound the shore, the great bear will come out to feed. Unless, like the lighthouse keeper and the keeper's family, you have strong walls and a heavy door protecting you, you are in peril for your life.

You will not hear the bear approaching. You will only hear the waves. You cannot run and hide.

Only I can save you. If the roar of the great lake's pounding surf seems to be moving, coming closer and closer to where you are, call out my name. Cry out, "DEREK, DELIVER ME!" and I will turn the bear aside. Remember my name and those words. They will be your only hope.

# THE LOGGING CAMP
## A TETTEGOUCHE STATE PARK
## GHOST STORY

L AST WINTER, WHEN MY two sons, Christopher and Jason, and I went snowshoeing in Tettegouche State Park near Silver Bay, we stayed in a cabin that was part of a logging camp built almost 100 years ago. On one of our hikes we came across the wreckage of what must have been one of the first cabins. It looked like it had been abandoned and left to ruin. We took some pictures and went on our way. Later, though, when Jason and Chris were taking the trail to Mt. Baldy, I decide to return to the site to poke through the collapsed cabin. I was looking for something to take home as a souvenir of our trip. What I found was a metal box that had been sealed shut with pine tar. Breaking through the tar and opening the box I found inside an envelope with writing across in large block letters. WARNING, it said, ON MOON-LESS NIGHTS: BEWARE!

Being curious, I returned to our cabin, put a few pieces of wood in the stove to keep me comfortable and, sitting down, opened the envelope, wanting to learn if anything inside explained the warning written outside. What was inside were several folded pages. I spent the afternoon copying them.

The original message, with its envelope and container, I brought to the park office. When the

ranger at the desk read the message on the envelope, his reaction was, frankly, terrifying. I had never seen anyone look so frightened. Then he shook himself, as though he was trying to wake up from a bad dream.

"This must be someone's idea of a joke," he said, choking on the words and ruining his attempt to make his comment sound casual and lighthearted. Then he gathered the material and laid it on his desk. "I'll keep this," he told me. "It's best that nothing be said about it. Stories like this might hurt attendance at the park."

So far as I know, the material I gave him has been destroyed or put away somewhere inaccessible to the public. Feeling he would take the copy from me, I said nothing about it. I share it with you for your own protection. On moonless nights, beware!

Your Friend
Gary W. Fehring

MAXWELL LAKE
JULY 23RD, 1911

My name is Sarah Hathaway. When you read these pages I will be dead. I accept my death, as terrible as I know it will be, as a punishment for what I have done. Although what I write here is not offered as an excuse for my actions, I believe when you read it you will understand that the evil I have done was in return for evil done to me.

Tonight there will be no moon. Tonight the instrument of my punishment will come for me. It is my hope that my death will put to final rest that thing which moves among the trees and brush on moonless nights. I leave this story should it be otherwise. Take no chances. If it is a moonless night when this is read, leave at once. When there is no moon, there is no safe place in this forest.

I came here from Chicago, intending to take over the logging business left to me by my uncle Maxwell. My uncle had gone west as a young man and made his fortune by working himself up from a simple lumberjack to the owner of a prosperous business in a remote area of the state of Minnesota. I was his only heir and though, being a woman and thinking myself unfit to manage an unruly crowd of tough men, which I assumed loggers to be, I decided to accept the challenge to come to Minnesota and make my future in its forest.

Armed with the deed and the not insignificant amount of money that came with it, I arrived in Duluth and made my way by hired coach to the fishing village of Beaver Bay where the manager of the camp had suggested I meet him. Mr. Lansford was the man's name. He was an older man, I judged, in his middle fifties. His welcome was warm and seemed genuine. Although there was a significant difference in our ages, his manner made him appear quite attractive to me, a thirty-year-old woman well on her way to becoming an old maid.

The logging camp was not easily accessible, but from his glowing reports I came to understand that it was doing very well with him managing its affairs. I could have a good life for myself. I felt lucky indeed to own so fine a business and for having such a capable and courteous man as he to look after it on my behalf.

While arrangements were being made to transport me the eight miles from Beaver Bay to the camp, Mr. Lansford took me to the bank where I deposited my inheritance in an account which, for business reasons, he suggested should be made out in his name. The deed, too, was redrawn replacing my name with that of Mr. Lansford.

You may ask why I did what must seem a very foolish thing. The reason was that he had spoken of marriage and, so far from home and in so sparsely populated and lonely a place, I deeply craved the companionship he offered.

The day chosen for our excursion to the camp was a Saturday morning. We traveled in his buggy, first along the shore of Lake Superior, then along a narrow and rugged path that took us deep into the forest and through dark and seemingly unfriendly hills. The journey took the entire day. Mr. Lansford had packed a lunch, and in a clearing by the bubbling water of a spring, we sat beneath the pines and enjoyed a delicious meal together. I remember it so well since it was the last experience unmixed with pain I was to know in life.

I made a gasp of joy when I caught first sight of my uncle's logging camp. There were several large buildings and one small charming cabin, all overlooking a very pretty lake. Mr. Lansford told me the lake had the indian name of Mic Mac but was known to the loggers as Lake Maxwell after my uncle.

When we entered the camp area, I commented that the place seemed deserted. Mr. Lansford told me that, as it was Saturday night, the crew had gone into town to enjoy themselves. When I wondered why they had not passed us along the way, he explained that there was a closer town north and east of camp. There the crew spent their weekly wages on alcohol and feminine entertainment. I clung more tightly to Mr. Lansford's arm when I realized what that latter activity might mean for me when they returned to camp. Mr. Lansford smiled at me and promised that I needed fear nothing from the loggers. It was one of the few thing he told me that was true. In all the years I have been here, no logger has ever bothered me.

Upon reaching the little cabin, Mr. Lansford tied the horse to the porch railing, helped me down from the buggy and told me that this would be my home when I was at the camp. In this cabin, he said, I would spend the night. He would use the bunk in one of the larger buildings where he had an office.

Because darkness was quickly gathering, Mr. Lansford lit a lantern. With that in hand and me on his arm, he led me through the cabin's door. How shocked I was to see by lantern light that everything within the cabin was covered with a thick coating of dust. When I asked why that should be, Mr. Lansford explained that the cabin had not been occupied since my uncle's death some two years before. In the morning, he said, we could make a game of cleaning and getting everything fit for my habitation. It would be fun, he said. And when the men returned later in the day we would have a party.

It was warm, so there was no need to build a fire. By lantern light we opened drawers and brought out bedding. I wiped up what dust I could from the table, bed and chamber pot beneath, while Mr. Lansford pumped a bucket of water, which he then poured into a basin and a pitcher so that I could both drink and wash. After acting upon my suggestion that he take the lantern and check the cabin through and through for any woodland creatures that might have found a home there, Mr. Lansford assured me I was quiet alone. With a tender kiss, he bid me good night.

I knew I should not be frightened, but I was. The cabin was secure. The lock was strong. There was oil enough to keep the lantern lit until morning. Still, I wished Mr. Lansford would have stayed there with me, if only such a thing were proper, which, not yet yoked in bonds of matrimony, it most certainly was not.

You must be sure, the night was difficult. From time to time I would drift off to sleep only to be harshly awaked by sounds that echoed loudly through the darkness.

The howling of the wolves, which, having lived till then in the city of Chicago, I was far from accustomed to, scared me. Once, heavy steps I imagined to be those of a bear thumped in several circles outside the cabin's walls. I retained a sense of calm by reminding myself of the cabin's stout construction and the knowledge that Mr. Lansford was not far away and would respond with haste in any emergency.

Had I known the latter was *not* true, I might well have died of fright. For among the many sounds that filled the forest darkness were those of a horse's movements and the squeaking of buggy's wheels. Mr. Lansford had abandoned me.

That I learned only at first light when, after washing and dressing as best I could amid the cabin's filth, I opened the door and saw that the horse and buggy were no longer there. My first thought was that Mr. Lansford had moved them into a stable somewhere on the property.

There was no answer when I called out Mr. Lansford's name. I smiled when I made a decision to wake this sound-sleeping fellow with a kiss. How surprised he would be.

It was I, though, who was surprised. Not so surprised as dismayed. Mr. Lansford was nowhere to be found. My first thought was that perhaps he had some business to attend to elsewhere in the area and would soon return. That hope was dashed by what I saw during my search. By day I could see that the camp had been long abandoned. There would be no loggers coming back to work that Sunday evening. I was totally alone and, except for a few days, would remain so for the rest of my life.

I did nothing for that entire day except return to my bed and lose myself in tears that would not stop. The man who caught my heart had lied to me. He did not love me. From the first, his intent had been only to seize my inheritance. His kindness had been a sham. What a fool I had been.

Day and night and day again, and I had neither ate nor drank. As for eating, the monster Lansford had left me nothing. He not only felt no love for me, he wanted me to die. He was convinced that, alone in the wilderness, this silly city woman would surely die of starvation.

Then, I thought, I wouldn't let that happen. I might have grown up in the city, but that did not mean I wasn't strong and resourceful. I would find a way to live if only for the single reason to thwart the purposes of the vile blackguard who sought to leave me in this place to die.

I'm sure you would tell me that all I had to do to save myself was return to Beaver Bay. I had but to follow the road that had brought us to the camp. I attempted to do just that. Remember, though, this had been a logging camp. The single ruts that served as road through the center of the camp became many. As often as I picked and chose, the choices I made led me nowhere except more deeply into the woods and hills. All that kept me from becoming lost and dying then and there was my making sure that Lake Maxwell was never far from sight.

Two days I spent seeking safe exit, until I was faint from hunger. To take more than the fewest of steps left me exhausted. What strength remained I used to search the camp for anything to aid my survival. There were axes and saws aplenty, but, for the moment, they had no usefulness for me. What I did find useful was a box of long abandoned fishing tackle.

I may have grown up a city girl, but the city I grew up in was on a lake. I knew of fishing. Fishing was what I did. The fish I caught I ate. At first I consumed them raw. When my fitness began to return, I cooked them on a spit I fashioned over an outdoor fire.

In the surrounding forest berries of several varieties had come in season. Some I knew from shopping at the market: raspberries, blueberries, in a patch some gooseberries. As I hunted through the brush, I discovered what had once been a garden, perhaps my uncle's garden. Still growing beneath the heavy brush which protected them from winter's freezing temperature were potatoes, onions, and carrots.

All these things I tended with such dedication that they have nourished me for all these many years. As for meat, I had neither skill nor implements for hunting. What I found was wire, which, in the winter, when I was able to trace rabbit trails, I fashioned into snares. In the summer I listened to the wolves and followed their howls to steal remnants of their kills. What they left, I ate. Its foul look and smell gave me a hunger for something fresh.

At first I meant to regain my strength only to make more attempts to return to civilization. The sun's path across the sky enabled me to establish east and west, north and south, as directions. Sighting from the shore of Maxwell Lake I noted landmarks in three of these directions. Should I climb to the top of the hills which lay to the south I could, I was certain, see Lake Superior and the road to Beaver Bay.

What would happen when I got there? Few people knew me. All that was legal was of benefit to the man who wronged me. I had no money to hire the professional help I would need to prove my case against my hated enemy. He would look at me and laugh. That, I could not bear.

*What was the hurry?* I told myself. This logging camp was mine. I was discovering the means I needed to survive. Mr. Lansford had left me here to die. My revenge would be to prove how wrong he was. I would grow both in my strength and in my hatred as to become the stuff of the nightmares I willed for him to have.

So passed the weeks, then months, then seasons, then years. Five years in all I spent beyond the sound of any human voice other than my own. Then, one afternoon, I did hear voices, sounds of horses and sounds of men. They were not far away and traveling in the direction of the camp. I was in the garden at the time and moved to take shelter behind the stable until I ascertained whether it was safe for my presence to be disclosed.

When I saw the horse in the lead, and the man who was riding on it, I knew it was not safe. The man was Mr. Lansford, five years older and much fatter than last I had seen him.

"There are some squatters here," he shouted to the men behind him. "I'll see to it they're gone before you buy the property."

With that the men dismounted and toured the buildings. From the cabin I heard Mr. Lansford laughing and cursing and smashing what I knew to be those few things—simple treasures I had gathered to brighten my daily living. Then I understood what I must do. If you have the courage to read on I will relate to you what that was.

The other men seemed upset by Mr. Lansford's extraordinary behavior. They left the cabin in haste and walked quickly toward the lake, discussing, I supposed, their plans to make the purchase of his property.

As Mr. Lansford continued his tirade , storming around the cabin and from time to time calling out my name, I made my way across the camp, easily avoiding the others. Before I reached the cabin I picked up the maul I had been using earlier to split wood to cook my evening meal.

Five years previous I could barely lift the heavy instrument. Since then it had grown lighter in my hands. Now I could swing it with ease for hours at a time.

One swing, though, would be all I would need. I would not use the bladed end. Although I had no reservation about leaving Mr. Lansford dead, it would not serve me well to have his body discovered by the others. Within months of his death, the logging camp would surely pass into their hands. That, I did not want. This place was mine, my home. I was determined never to leave. Never!

Mr. Lansford must disappear. The camp could be neither bought nor sold in his absence. Unable to purchase the property in any timely manner, surely those men seeking to acquire it would lose interest, and the logging camp would be forgotten, as it had been for so many years.

Upon reaching the cabin, I saw that the door had been left open with Mr. Lansford inside, muttering that he would find me. When he left this time, he said, I would not be left alive. Leaving the maul beside the door, I went round to a back window where I stood and called his name.

"Mr. Lansford, darling, you have come back for me. I have waited so long to become your bride."

Hearing him move toward the window I fairly flew back to the cabin's door, taking my place hidden in its shadow, the maul held high above my head.

When Mr. Lansford came out, thinking, I am sure, to find me and to kill me, I struck him, and he fell. The wire for my snares was close at hand.

I trussed him with it, gagged him with the scarf I had been wearing on my head, and carried him into the forest where I left him.

Little time had passed for all this to be done. The other men had remained by the lake. Good, I thought. Mounting Mr. Langsford's horse, I snapped the reins and used my heels. We left the camp at a gallop.

I have but one regret about the actions of that day. I had to kill Mr. Lansford's horse. Leading the poor animal off the path, I tied the reins to a tree and slit its throat.

At any other time I would have butchered the fallen body for its meat. For the moment I had another addition to my diet in mind. The flesh of the horse would be long spoiled when I had need of it. I had laid aside what would serve me for many meals, and would stay fresher in the summer's heat.

Hearing the hoof beats of the horse, and finding Mr. Lansford gone, the others left, as I knew they would. Alone, again, in the logging camp, I made arrangements for Mr. Lansford's return. In one of the buildings I knew there to be a stout chair which would serve my purpose. Then I filled a box with torn pieces of sheets and clothes, which had been left behind long ago.

To spare your sensibilities I will not describe in detail that which took place in what was left of

Mr. Lansford's life as a human being and a food supply.

The man was awake when I carried him out of the forest. How he squirmed. There was such a frenzied look in his eyes when I embraced him and told him how happy I was to know how much he loved me. This very day, I told him, we would be married.

I had been to weddings and remembered a few things from them. I told Mr. Lansford that I took him for my husband; for better, for worse, for richer, for poorer, to love and to cherish, till death us do part. Then it was Mr. Lansford's turn. I asked him if he took me for his wife. When I removed the gag so he could answer he only screamed. I took that for a yes.

The exchange of rings could have been a problem. I had no ring for him, but I saw he had one for me. With a shears I cut off Mr. Lansford's ring finger, removed what was on it and, slippery as it was with blood, slid the ring on the third finger of my left hand.

I was glad that before I carried out that act I had replaced the gag. I was also pleased that I had been prudent enough to find the chair in which I had tied him. Any other would have broken to pieces, so mightily did my new husband struggle.

That very evening, we consummated our union by becoming one. Like the ring, it could not be done in the usual way. What I did was consume a slice I took from the calf of his leg. I made a fire and cooked it before his eyes.

Our marriage lasted for about a week as I cut the flesh, bound the wounds and cooked the meat, always accompanying my efforts to maintain our oneness with many tender kisses. I believe Mr. Lansford understood my intent and grew to love me. What has happened since, on every moonless night, has convinced me of that.

After the week, our marriage ended. Death parted us. The meat I was eating began to spoil. What was left of Mr. Lansford—and despite my healthy appetite, there was still a considerable amount—I brought out to the forest for the dining pleasure of those whose taste was not as refined as my own. It was dark when I returned to camp. It was a moonless night.

When I am writing this many years have passed. I have remained here alone, alone, except for my darling husband. I hear him every moonless night. He walks toward me through the woods. "It's dinner time, my beloved," I hear him say. "Are you hungry? I am hungry, too."

Each moonless night I hear him outside my cabin door. On the next night when there is no moon, I will open that door and allow him to come in. Perhaps, then, Mr. Lansford's hunger will be satisfied. If it is not, there'll be nowhere safe on those nights without a moon. Knowing Mr. Lansford, he will walk some distance for a meal.

# THE LODGE

## A SCENIC STATE PARK GHOST STORY

That's me you're looking at. I'm the guy in the middle. Next to me on the left is Bill from Waterloo, Iowa. Next to him is Jack from Green Bay. On my right are two brothers, Joe and Sam, local guys from Grand Rapids. They're dead, all four of them. I should say all five of us. I'm dead, too. Have been for a long time, probably since before you were born.

Let me tell you some things. Some of the things you know. One, you don't. You and your family are camping at Scenic State Park by Big Fork, Minnesota. You know that. You're standing in the lodge at the Lodge Campground. You're looking at pictures of the guys who built that lodge. That's all stuff you know. The thing you don't know is that while you are looking at me, I am looking at you.

Don't let that scare you. It's day time, and I don't have my pick ax with me. I only carry that at night. I'll have it tonight.

I'm good with that pick ax. I got a lot of practice with it when the other guys in those pictures and I built this lodge and the other stuff in this park. I'll bet you don't know that this park was famous. Newspapers as far away as New York City printed stories about how great a place this was when we got done with it.

It's still a great place. That's not why I stay around. I'm here because I got a score to settle. I guess I'm a ghost. Back before I was a ghost that's what I'd have called myself, like in, "Hey, I seen a ghost." There are a lot of ghosts around, but I'm the only one here at the park. Us ghosts all have this in common. We are what we are and where we are because we each have a score to settle.

My beef is with the guy in the picture to your left, the guy carrying that log. He's the guy who killed me.

I suppose you know all about the CCC; the Civilian Conservation Corps. That's what we were when we built this park. We did that' during the Depression. Those days guys like me didn't have no jobs. Knowing that it ain't good to have a bunch of guys around with nothing to do but make trouble, one of the first things President Roosevelt did after he got to be president was put us to work out in the woods.

Before I joined the CCC, the closest I ever was to any woods was the tree behind the shack we lived in where I used to go to take a piss. That shack was in a place called Swede Hollow in St. Paul. Where we lived wasn't far from Johnson High School, but I never went there. A lot of my buddies in the Corps quit school after eighth grade. I didn't last that long. By the time I finished sixth grade, I'd had enough of school, and school had more than enough of me.

If the Corp hadn't come along I would probably have spent the rest of my life in the Ramsey County jail, which wouldn't have been much better than spending it where I did, under the ground here at the park.

I almost didn't get in the Corps. If the doctor hadn't given me a break, I would have flunked the physical. That's how skinny and sickly looking I was. I'm not that way anymore, and it was the Corps that made the difference. I never loved anything, even my folks, as much as I loved the CCC. It made me strong. More than that it made me feel like I was important and could do important things, like building the lodge you're standing in. Ain't this a great place? After all these years it's just as great a place as when we built it and those New York papers wrote about it.

Building this park I felt good about myself and good about what I was doing. For the first time in my life I had buddies I could trust, and who trusted me. The guys in charge were veterans, most of them, soldiers who'd fought in the First World War. They worked us hard, but they were fair, and they didn't treat me like the weasel I had been in Swede Hollow. They gave me the chance to earn their respect. I took that chance and ran with it.

Working here, building the lodge, the shelters, the trails, and the campsites, I came to understand that the trees were not just here for me to piss on. They are here for me to wonder at. These pines in Scenic Park are everything I wanted to be—tall, strong, something other people admired instead of pissing on.

Being in Corps, working here in the park, was the best time of my life. It stayed that way until Andrew Fisher, Jr., showed up.

Like me Andrew came from St. Paul, but from a different part of town, up on Summit Avenue a block or two away from the cathedral. Before his folks lost their money in the Depression, they had been rich, and Andrew, Jr., not only graduated from high school, he had been a Eagle Scout. Just to show how much better than the rest of us he was, the son of a b_ _ _h tacked his eagle badge and sash full of merit badges on the wall above his cot.

Doing that made junior a joke to the rest of us. We had plenty of fun with his trophies. I don't think he could ever have gotten the stains out of that merit badge sash after we left it soaking in the latrine. Doing that wasn't right. It made me feel bad about myself for the first time since I joined the CCC.

What was right was when one of the guys who worked in the shop made a swastika out of a couple of nails, and we attached it to the eagle on his badge. We all got in trouble for that, but we knew it was the right thing to have done. Andrew Fisher, Jr., was a nazi.

He wasn't a real nazi, but he would have been if he had been living in Germany. His badges wouldn't have come from the Boy Scouts. He would have gotten them from the Hitler Youth. We came to call him Adolph, Jr., because he bragged about how great a leader Adolph Hitler was. Being in the Corps, FDR was our hero. To Adolph, Jr., Roosevelt was just a commie Jew lover. Junior hated Roosevelt and he hated Jews.

There was one Jew in our camp. His name was David Rothstein, and Adolph, Jr.,hated him. The way he treated David Rothstein gave the whole camp a bad feeling.

Adolph, Jr., was bigger than David Rothstein. He was bigger and meaner than any of the others guys in the camp. That's why we could never challenge him or let him know who was messing with his stuff. We were all on one side. Andrew Fisher, Jr., was on the other. David Rothstein was in the middle.

It was like Adolph, Jr., was trying to prove his loyalty to his *fuhrer* by making the life of this one Jew miserable. Somehow, whatever Adolph, Jr., was working with had a way of doing damage to David. The shovel handle would hit him. Boiling water would splash on him. Cement dust would blow up into David's eyes. The canoe paddle would hit him in the head. When those things happened, the rest of us just sat back and watched.

The only time Junior got into trouble for the way he was treating Rothstein was when he told the kid he was going to have to greet him with the nazi salute. One of the veterans, who had come back from whipping the Germans in the war, overheard what Andrew said and kicked him so hard in the ass that he couldn't sit down for a week.

For about two month Adolph, Jr., kept riding Rothstein until the kid couldn't take it anymore and left the camp. I hate to say it, but in a way I wish Junior would have killed Rothstein, or that Rothstein would have committed suicide here at the camp. Then I would have his ghost to keep me company. Maybe, though, that would not have been such a great idea. Rothstein's ghost would probably have a score to settle with me because I never stood up for him. I didn't have the guts to do that then. I try to make up for that by doing it now.

As a ghost I have a score to settle with Adolph, Jr., the guy who killed me. He's never come back here to the park, and early on I discovered I can't leave. All I can do is hope that when he left here his dream came true and he got to Germany and became a real nazi. Then, maybe, Rothstein's dream, and the dream of the rest of us in the camp came true and Andrew Fisher, Jr., met some people tougher than he was at Stalingrad.

Like I said, all us ghosts have a score to settle. I can see mine being settled for me by a Russian trooper with a good sharp bayonet. What I'm doing is settling the score for what happened to David Rothstein here at the park. When anyone comes along who treats other people the way Adolph, Jr., treated David Rothstein, I've got my pick ax, and I'm ready for them. If that's the kind of person you are, let me tell you how I am going to know.

HOW I'M GOING TO KNOW has to do with how I got to be a ghost. Adolph, Jr., took care of that by hitting me in the back with my own pick ax. He drove it clean through me until the last thing I saw was the point coming out my chest. What happened was that while I was cleaning up around the bunks I saw something sticking out

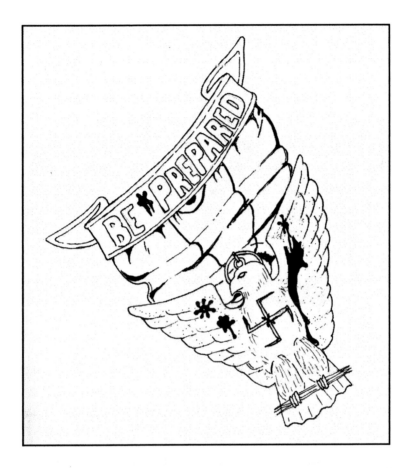

from under Adolph's mattress. It was a pair of women's panties. Our Aryan superman was a pervert. Before the day was over, everyone in camp was going to know it.

Or, they would have if Andrew hadn't come in while I was looking at the panties. I think he must have realized he hadn't put his treasure out of sight and came back to fix that. When he saw me, and what I had in my hand, he grabbed the pick ax I'd left by the door and used it to keep his secret.

Just that quick, part of me was dead, but, with a score to settle, and I had one, another part of me became what I am now. I watched what the guy who killed me did with what he must of thought was all of me, but was only the part of me that was dead.

There was a place in the park where we had started to dig a well, but the plans had changed. The hole we'd dug hadn't been filled in yet so Adolph, Jr., tossed me in and covered me up with the dirt. When he was done, he started laughing. Standing on my grave, packing the dirt with his feet, he laughed.

The next day, Adolph, Jr., left the CCC. There was about a week or so when the guys tried to find where I might have gone. Of course they never did. Over time, the place Adolph, Jr., stuck me just became part of the landscape of the park. You couldn't find it if you tried.

I know where it is. The score I have to settle is with the person who stands on that spot and laughs. I'll use on them the same pick ax that was used me. So, if you think it's okay to treat people like you are better than them, be careful where you walk.

# SARAH IN THE WATER

## A MONSON LAKE STATE PARK GHOST STORY

MONDAY, JULY 13TH, 2009
I'm getting old and my ears don't work so good. I hate to admit that, but it explains why I didn't hear the young lady before when she had spoken to me. It wasn't until last night that she spoke loud enough for me to catch what she was saying. It was difficult for her to speak loudly, she said, because of what the Sioux had done to her throat when they killed her.

She and her family lived here, the girl told me. Their house was close to the lake. That's where she was thrown, into the lake, after she was dead. The Sioux left the bodies of her parents and brothers in the house when they burned it down. When the neighbors didn't find her body they thought she had been taken captive. They never looked for her in the lake. That's what she had spent the last century and a half waiting for, for someone to find her and bury her in the church yard with her family. When I asked her why, in all this time, no one else had looked for her, the answer was that I was the first person she had spoken to. She noticed me, she said, because I seemed to be as lonely and alone as she.

I am alone. That's the way it has been all my life. God has put me in a world apart. It could not be more difficult for me to connect with other people if I lived with the fish on the bottom of Monson Lake.

That's where I am. That's where the girl told me her story, at Monson Lake, not in it. Minnesota has a state park here where I set up my tent. Every summer I came here for the fishing. The sunfish in Monson Lake are some of the biggest I'd ever seen. I came here to camp and fish. I came here alone.

Monson Lake State Park is a quiet place. It's a small park, and I'd never seen it crowded. Often, I was the only person in the campground. It was here at Monson Lake that a band of Sioux attacked and killed the girl and her family. It happened during the 1860s uprising, when the Native Americans took revenge on the white settlers for the shameful and shabby way they were being treated by the government.

There is a memorial here where the home once stood. Every time I came to Monson Lake I walked over and paid my respects. I understood the why, but not the what, of the behavior of the first Americans. It's the old story of the innocent taking the punishment of the guilty.

What the girl told me was not about punishment. It was about peace. It was about being at peace. It was about being in the company of those she had known and loved, those who had known and loved her.

I understood how she felt. For me life is as cold as the water of a Minnesota lake in early spring. While the word "warmth" is not the first that comes to mind when I think of the grave, I understand that a special kind of heat is generated by being close to those we love, even after death. Where, I think, will I find peace and warmth for my soul? There is a wall of ice as thick as that on any frozen lake between me and those whose lives I had once been part of. Once, perhaps, I could have found within me whatever was necessary to melt that ice. Not anymore. That was long ago. Whatever it may have been is no longer there.

She knew all that. Without being told, she knew it. It was as much for me as for herself that I was the one she chose. I was being asked to bring us both to a place neither she nor I could get to by ourselves.

Last night, in the dreamy darkness of my tent, as she spoke to me, it seemed so simple. When the morning came I would take my canoe into Monson Lake and there she would be. The two of us, each no longer alone, would journey to the church yard where I would bring her home.

Now, in the daylight, that simplicity is no longer there. Now there are no answers. Now there are only questions. Was the girl really there, or was it all a dream? If it wasn't a dream, if her spirit, or ghost, or whatever, had spoken to me, what then? Find her and bring her to the church yard? Easily said, but she had been in the lake for over a hundred years. What would I look for? What would I find?

What had been so beautiful in the disembodied dark had ghastly edges to it in the world of vision. I had planned to fish that day, but did I dare? If I should, when I felt something on the line and reeled in, would it be a swimming, spinning sunfish, or would I drag up something else?

There was too much here for me to deal with. I packed my things and left.

Tuesday, July 14th, 2009

Yesterday, I tried to leave, but something stopped me. What I tried to force myself to regard as nothing but a dream kept resisting my best efforts. Fear prevented me from venturing out onto the lake. It was accompanied by a strange tugging on my heart that held me in my place.

Alone in the campground I brought a chair to the fishing pier and spent the entire day looking at the water. Sunlight danced in shimmering sparkles from the wavelets called into being by a soft, soft breeze. On such a day could nature's beauty be corrupted by human ugliness? Did sunlight sparkle from the splashing circles spreading from where Sarah's body struck the surface of the lake? Was the water's clarity stained and clouded by the red, life blood that once belonged to Sarah but was no longer hers to keep?

That was, that is, her name. Her name is Sarah. Sarah spoke to me again last night. Last night she convinced me that as dreamlike as it is, what I was experiencing could never be a dream. You had to be asleep to dream. I spent last night awake. I was awake when Sarah spoke to me. I did not have to pinch myself to know it. I was in my chair on the fishing pier slapping mosquitoes.

If anyone had seen me, I'd have been taken for insane and been on my way for treatment at Willmar hospital. Sane people don't spend the night sitting in a chair on a fishing pier talking to someone who wasn't there.

That was what I did. That was what *we* did. We talked. We shared our stories. Our stories were far different. Considering when Sarah was born, you might expect her story to be the longest. It was not. Beyond death there is no passing time. There is only present experience, pain or peace, loneliness or love.

When I told my story, I realized it was the same for me. My story was not in the passing of days and happenings. Like Sarah, what I was and know was the pain of loneliness. What we longed for was not more mornings to wake up into, more days to walk through. All we wanted was to know peace and love. Forgetting the seventy-three years, five months, eleven days since my birth, the whole story of my life was that I was experiencing those very things last night sitting on my chair on the Monson Lake State Park fishing pier in the company of a girl whose story was much like my own.

Today I packed up. I had a lot to do, and the sooner I got at it, the sooner I'd get done.

Thursday, June 17th, 2010

I finished all I had to do. The last thing was to set up my tent in the Monson Lake State Park campground. It was evening, and I was on the lake in my canoe. The other fisherman had gone to shore. A storm was coming, and it was reported to be severe.

The storm wouldn't bother me. I would be beyond its reach before it hit. Today was Sarah's birthday. Deep in the lake she waited for me. Weighed down by the heavy clothes I was wearing, I would join her. The stories of two lonely lives would become one story. The peace and love so important for us both would be ours forever.

Saturday, June 19th, 2010
*The Willmar Tribune*
## ST. PAUL MAN DROWNS IN MONSON LAKE

On Friday the body of James Gerry of St. Paul, Minnesota, was recovered from Monson Lake. Campers at Monson Lake State Park reported that in spite of storm warnings Gerry had gone fishing in his canoe. "I told him about the storm," one camper said, "but I don't think he heard me."

A St. Paul neighbor confirmed that the victim had a hearing problem.

According to park officials, Gerry was a regular visitor to Monson Lake. His appreciation of the area was accepted as the reason that, even though he had no relatives in the area, he had arranged that he be buried in the cemetery at Monson Lake Lutheran Church. George Carlson, the funeral director handling the arrangements could not explain Gerry's request that the date of birth to be carved into the stone marking his grave be June 17th, 1845.

# The Thing in the Pool

## A Whitewater State Park Ghost Story

THE FLOOD INITIATED the chain of events setting it loose. In flood stage, the Whitewater River tore through its namesake park, ripping great gashes in State Highway 74 and digging deeply into every natural and manmade obstacle blocking its passage to the Mississippi.

What it did to the mound at the foot of Granddad Bluff was to scour it clean of centuries of soil and vegetation accumulated over the great pile of rocks, boulders, and limestone slabs forming its core. It was thought that the mound was a natural phenomenon, created by debris detached from the face of the cliff and fallen to the valley floor.

That supposition was in error. The mound was manmade. The Dakota, who lived and hunted in the shelter of the ancient bluffs, had expended huge effort to cover the thing they feared with a weight from which it would be unable to escape.

Natural or manmade, the exposed heap of stone was viewed as a godsend by the crews sent to repair the damage caused by the flooded river. Piece by piece, the pile was dismantled, its contents used for fill to restore the parkland and the highway running through it. When the excavation was complete, all that remained was the pool of water the stone heap had covered. In that pool of water, imprisoned for so many centuries, was the powerful and hostile being the Dakota had attempted to forever bury.

Where the thing in the pool came from, and what might be its nature doesn't really matter. Whether earthborn spirit, alien intruder, or discarded angel brought down from heaven with Lucifer's banishment, what matters most about it is that it tolerates no disturbance to its timeless contemplation of its own existence.

Having no needs or desires that could not be satisfied by its meditation upon itself, the ghost being allowed life in the valley to run its course unmolested. It was only when that self-centered bemusement was interrupted that the being's docile existence was altered. Across the millennia, the single cause that brought about that change in being from contemplative spirit to raging demon had been when stones from the bluff above become dislodged and fell into the water which was the being's home.

When that occured, its anger was aroused. Erupting ghostlike from the pool, it rushed to in habit the body of whatever warm-blooded being it first encountered. Given physical form, the thing brought about a fury of destruction in proportion to the size and strength of whatever animal it happened to inhabit.

After those occasions had passed, the valley floor was littered with the debris of the monster's devastation. Often such damage passed unnoticed should the pool thing have vented its wrath in one of the valley's smaller animals, a gopher, rabbit, squirrel, or such. Those times a larger form was occupied—a wolf, perhaps, or a bear— huge areas of ground were heaped with torn bodies left behind when the life form was finally vacated and the pool thing resumed the solitude it seemed condemned to so desperately require.

Unaware of the pool being's existence, a tribe of Dakota settled in the valley, finding it a pleasant place to hunt and live. Their first experience with what was in the pool came during a storm that dislodged a single stone. This stone tumbled down the cliffside, bouncing from one outcropping to another until it fell with a loud *kerplunk* into the water. One of the tribe's dogs, which happened to be drinking from the pool when the stone splashed in, raced back into the village barking, making what seemed like unearthly howls. Before the animal left, three families had been mutilated beyond recognition. The dog was finally killed where it was found, unconscious by the edge of the pool beneath the bluff.

Some thought the dog's maniacal behavior was the result of the disease which caused dogs' mouths to foam, although a careful examination of the carcass of the animal revealed no typical signs of such condition.

Others in the tribe believed the dog had been possessed by some evil spirit. They were closer to the truth. Considering that, the tribe's spiritual leaders outlined a series of dances and rituals to prevent a reoccurrence.

Neither the violence of the storm, nor the animal's proximity to the pool was regarded as significant. Then, one of the children, playing in the forest with his friends, threw a rock into the water.

According to what was described by the only survivor of what came next, the splash of the rock was followed by a disturbance that seemed to rise from deep within the pool. Reaching the surface, a ghostlike mist attacked the boy and transformed the otherwise quiet and well-mannered young man into something no longer human.

The lone survivor of the destruction that followed, a girl who had managed to find shelter behind a tree, watched as her playmates were pursued by the stone thrower. With a speed and strength that defied description, the boy caught and killed his former friends, one after another, ripping them apart with his bare hands and teeth. When there was no more damage to be done, the being that had taken over the boy led him back to the pool into which, after leaving his battered body behind, it returned.

The death of the stone-throwing boy—demanded by the grieving families of the children ho killod was forootalled by the surviving girl's story, which made it clear that something in the pool, not the boy, was responsible for the tragedy. To the relief of his parents, the possessed child recovered from his injuries. When questioned by his father, all he could say was that his only memory of what had taken place following his throwing a stone into the pool was the feeling of something like a snake swallowing him whole.

Having no choice except to believe the girl's story and the boy's description, the tribal leaders decided that whatever was living in the pool was beyond human understanding and beyond their ability to oppose. The most they could do was to declare the pool and the area surrounding it sacred ground, and no one in the village was allowed to go there.

Since the people in the village were terror-stricken by what had taken place with the dog and the boy, and horrified by the thought that such a thing could happen again, the warning to avoid the pool was unnecessary. No one would be so foolish as to go anywhere near that pool of water beneath the bluff.

No one did. Month's passed and although from time to time a rock would fall from somewhere above and rouse the fury of the thing in the pool, only small animals had been nearby, resulting in destruction, which was insignificant and unnoticed.

That changed in the spring when the ice, that during the winter shielded the thing in the pool from disturbance, melted from the pool and the cliffside. Rocks, formerly frozen in place, broke loose and tumbled to the valley floor, many of them striking the surface of the water, causing splashes that drove the being within into measureless fury.

A mother black bear, having emerged with her two cubs from winter's hibernation, was at the pool's edge when the ghost monster tore loose from the water and threw itself around her.

The first in the village to die was a brave who had been hunting in the forest between the village and the pool. He had been stalking a deer when the mother bear came upon him. Although the arrow meant for the deer drove into the bear's body, it caused no apparent damage. As the brave attempted to raise his bow for another shot, he was dealt a blow that drove him to the ground. By the time the mother bear continued on, what was left behind could hardly be described as having been human.

Before the day was out, everyone in the village unable to escape was dead. Only long after the screaming had stopped were those who had run for cover in the forest brave enough to return. What they found both sickened and enraged them. Children found their parents clawed and bitten. Brothers and sisters found their siblings gouged and torn. The ground was swimming in a sea of blood it was too saturated to absorb.

The ceremonies of commending the dead to the warm embrace of Mother Earth were hastily completed, and the decision was made that, for the protection of the village, and in honor of those who had died, revenge must be taken on the being beneath the surface of the pool.

They would bury it. They would bury it all at once. It could be done. Hanging above the pool was a great outcropping of rock split away from the body of the bluff halfway from the summit to the valley floor. Although a substantial effort would be required, the tribal leaders believed the hold of the outcropping to the bluff could be broken. When that happened, the freed material would fall into the pool directly beneath, burying, it was hoped, the being within so deeply it could never get out.

The work of breaking the outcropping loose was begun as trees were felled and huge levers shaped, carried up the bluff and set in place. Aware that rocks would fall into the pool while this was being done, the village was moved to the shores of the Mississippi River. To protect themselves from any mayhem that might occur below, those who stayed to carry out the work spent as little time as possible on the valley floor, eating and sleeping in a shelter they had put together on the top of the bluff.

During the weeks of making ready for the burial of the thing in the pool the tribe's only encounter with the monster's fury occurred when a rock fell into the water after having been knocked loose by the emplacement of a log lever. The next moment an eagle, feeding nearby on the remains of a gopher, became the terrible being's chosen instrument.

Striking one of the workers in the face, the eagle tore out his eyes. While the bird's talon were sunk into his flesh the man, aware of what would happen to his companions when the eagle finished with him, grabbed the eagle's legs. Holding them with all his strength, the suffering brave dove from the bluff top. The two of them, eagle and man, plummeted to the earth, striking the pool with a great splash and disappearing beneath its surface.

Looking down from far above, the workers watched as the splashes made by falling stones were followed by a displacement of water as though something from deep within the earth was forcing itself to the surface. For an instant a vortex of swirling mist hovered over the disturbance in the water. Then it was gone. What the workers could not see was the horror being inflicted beneath the forest's foliage. Huge gashes were torn as the ghost creature, under a near constant state of agitation, ran rampant, invading one animal after another until all that remained in the area were rotting corpses.

Unsure of what might happen to themselves, and the world as they knew it, if the demon spirit was out of the pool when the rocks fell to bury it, the Dakota workers prepared everything so that all that remained holding the pillar-like outcropping in place was the stone at its base. There they set their levers. When what was needed was in place they halted every movement for an entire day, insuring as best they could that nothing would fall into the water and drive the ghost mist out.

The thing in the pool did not experience the passage of time. It neither knew nor cared about what was happening in the world above. All it experienced was solitude or disturbance. When the levers of the Dakota were moved and the tons of rock were dropped, the disturbance that broke the being's solitude led to an outburst of hostility which had heretofore been assuaged by an attack on the world above.

Prevented from doing so again, the ghost thing resumed the meditation which, under its ice-like shield of rock, had gone on, undisturbed, until the present.

The Dakota returned their village to its former location near the buried pool where they lived their lives in peace until the arrival of the Europeans. Driving the first inhabitants from their land, the Europeans took their place, building their homes along the waterways of the Mississippi and its tributaries.

All this meant nothing to the being beneath the rocks. When the Europeans, who had grown to call themselves Americans, created a park around the being's place of residence, the ghost thing took no notice. The floods that came and went, as powerful as they were, caused no movement in the great heap of rock that protected it from experiencing anything except itself.

So long had been its isolation from environmental intrusions, and so deep its introspection on its own existence, that it failed to be aroused by the construction crew's removal of the covering rock.

Then, as the dripping of a leaky faucet creates a growing irritation in a person seeking a good night's sleep, the return of the nuisance of debris falling from the top and sides of Granddad Bluff restored the being's former temper.

Whitewater State Park in Southeastern Minnesota is a wonderful place to visit. Since the property has recovered from the damage done by the flood of a few years ago, the park is a great place to camp. Should you do so, choose a campsite as far distant as possible from the pool at the foot of Granddad Bluff. While the view from the top of the bluff is most exhilarating and worth the effort of the climb, as you negotiate the trail be careful not to dislodge any rocks along the trail's outer edge. Should one of them fall into the pool, there's no telling what you will find when you return to the valley floor.

# THE EMPTY CHAIR

## A SAKATAH LAKE STATE PARK GHOST STORY

T HAT WAS SOMETHING we didn't expect to see. It would have been okay if we had been in Calcutta, but we weren't. We were in the Bullhead Capital of the World, Sakatah Lake State Park, Waterville, Minnesota, just about as far away as one can get from the Indian subcontinent. We didn't expect to see it, but there it was. There *she* was.

What one might expect to see at Sakatah Lake are hikers, bikers, bird lovers, bullhead lovers, tree huggers, and the usual assortment of uniformed juveniles—cub, boy, girl, and so on. The woman sitting on the chair didn't seem to fit into any of those categories. If she had, we wouldn't have noticed her or been so creeped out by what we were seeing.

It wasn't only the *sari* in which she was wrapped that seemed so unnatural, given the setting. If she had been reading a book, or toasting marshmallows, or even swatting mosquitos, we would have waved and called out a greeting as camping neighbors should. Instead, the woman was sitting, unmoving, in the chair, staring at apparently nothing. Although there was no visible evidence, I assumed the woman was alive, but, for all I knew, she could have been a figure delivered to the park from some local wax museum.

Maybe, if it been a weekend and the park had been crowded with people, the sight of the woman would not have been so unnerving. As it was, it was midweek, and the place was pretty much deserted. Where we were spending the night, the cabin on the far end of the campground, was especially isolated. None of us was able to shake the unsettled feeling brought on by the sight of the woman on the chair and the aloneness of our situation.

When I say, we, I mean my son and daughter and myself. Working weekends, and with only a couple of days off midweek, we were taking a quick camping trip to a park close to our home in Minneapolis. Sakatah Lake State Park, an hour's drive away, fit the bill. The availability of its single camper cabin clinched the deal.

It was after we registered and were driving through the campground to the cabin that, passing an otherwise empty parking lot, we saw the woman sitting on the chair. From that moment on the three of us had the feeling that something about her being there was wrong. While no one suggested we should return the cabin key to the park office and head back home, we were all silently considering that option. When, after unloading the car and setting up in the cabin, we drove back to the park office for wood to cook supper, we realized that's what we should have done, packed up, turned around and gone home. Passing the parking lot we saw that the woman was gone. All that remained was the empty chair.

I should tell you that, despite being a fine place to camp and having excellent bike and hiking trails, Sakatah Lake is not one of Minnesota's primer state parks. During the week, the office closes at 3:00 p.m. Even if we had wanted to do so, there was no one we could ask about who that woman was, and why she had been sitting on that chair in that empty parking lot.

Camping together there was always plenty to talk about, but our conversation kept returning to the woman and the empty chair. I suggested that perhaps the rest of her family had gone fishling and she was practicing some sort of Hindu meditation while she waited for them. That explained everything except while, after they collected her, they had left behind the chair. There could, of course, have been all sorts of reasons for that, none of them particularly sinister. They could simply have forgotten the chair, or considered it of no value. It might not even have belonged to them. Whatever the reason, the empty chair lost its significance when, as we drove to the fishing pier to spend the evening, we saw that, like the woman who had been sitting in it, the chair was gone.

On our trip into Waterville to buy firewood we loaded up with worms and minnows, intending to bait our hooks with meals the local fish population would find irresistible. What looked so delicious to us (from a fish's point of view) did not prove to be so.

We might have been casting our lines into the waters of the Bullhead Capital of the World, but you couldn't prove it by us. Our practice of catch and release was sometimes tested by our bringing in what, if my wife allowed, would look good on our living room wall. No problem that night. The few sunfish that dined on our worms were full of vim and vigor, and cute as buttons, but hardly bigger than the bait they were attempting to consume.

Our poor luck on the fishing pier was no cause for disappointment. We had fun being together. Another plus was that the activity provided other things to think about and talk about than the woman in the chair. Driving back to the cabin bought such distractions to an abrupt conclusion. There was no woman in the empty parking lot, but the chair was back exactly where it had been, facing the road as though something unseen was sitting there staring at us and through us.

I don't know if it would have been more disturbing if the woman, whoever or whatever she was, had been back. I suppose it would have. Still, the empty chair was bad enough. If it was back, she was back. If she wasn't in the chair, where was she? What if what she'd been staring at, and what seemed by the sight of it to have frozen her in place, was more unnatural, more disturbing, than the woman herself?

Our family is not a superstitious bunch. Although we had sat together through many a horror film, from *Frankenstein* and *Dracula* to the Hawk's and Carpenter's versions of *The Thing*, none of us really believed there were such beings as ghosts, alien monsters, or the undead. We knew there had to be some rational explanation for the empty chair and the strange appearance and behavior of the woman who had been sitting on it.

We knew that, but we still couldn't shake the feeling that something around us was wrong. This park, on this night, was not a safe place for us to be. Had we been staying in a tent, I doubt any of us would have even thought of sleeping. The cabin, though, brought a stronger sense of security. It had electric lights, a good stout door that could be locked, sturdy walls and modern, well-fitting windows. Nothing could get in at us.

There was, however, one thing the cabin did not have. It did not have a toilet. The closest facilities provided for such purposes was a pit toilet about a hundred yards away through the trees. My son and I did not find that situation disadvantageous. When we had to, we could step outside and tend to business within a step or two of the safety of the cabin door. My daughter, though, would have none of that. When nature called, she would take the required excursion.

As I have made clear, we didn't believe in ghosts. There was no reason going to the outdoor toilet should be scary. Not doing it would be an admission of weakness and stupidity. My son and I would have done it, we told ourselves, if we had to. We just didn't have to. The time came, though, when my daughter had to. The last thing she said as she left the cabin was, "If I see that woman, I don't know what I'll do. I'll probably die of fright."

I guess that was what happened. We don't know what she saw, whether it was the woman or the thing the woman had been staring at. What happened was, she didn't come back. After waiting far longer than we should have, my son and I grabbed our flashlights and took off looking for her.

When we called her name, there was no answer. When we stopped and listened, there was no sound, no call for help, nothing but silence. Near the pit toilet we found her flashlight lying in the underbrush beside the trail, still lit. With that, my son used his cell phone to call for help.

By the time law enforcement arrived, we were frantic. On foot and using the searchlights on their vehicles, the police scoured the park. There was no sign of her. The next day, volunteers from the local community, along with dogs brought in from the Twin Cities, discovered only where she had been, not where she was. Two days spent with divers and drag lines searching the lake were no more successful.

Grief could not be denied. My wife and I faced the terrible, terrible truth that our beloved little girl was gone. We knew she hadn't run away. Perhaps she had been taken by some pervert. That would have been the worst thing—taken, molested, murdered, dumped somewhere like garbage. Unlike my wife, who found that the most likely cause of her sudden disappearance, I knew that hadn't happened. Ours was the only vehicle in the park. Even had we been unable to see anything in the dark, the night had been so quiet we would certainly have heard something driving away.

A few weeks later I returned alone to Sakatah Lake State Park. I don't know why I went, or what I expected to find, I just had the feeling I had to go. No one wanted to go with me. My son would never return to that place. My wife has never seen it, and never will.

That is just as well. In that park is the stuff of madness. As I drove the road toward the cabin in which we had stayed I passed the parking lot. Once again it was empty, except for the chair. Sitting on the chair was the woman in the Indian *sari*. As before, she sat unmoving, staring into the distance. Slowing down as I passed I recognized who the woman was. She was my daughter. By the time I stopped the car and ran to the parking lot, all I found was the empty chair.

Now, every year I spend a few days by myself at Sakatah Lake State Park. Our daughter is always there when I arrive. As before, when I get to her, all that remains is the empty chair. I sit where she had been and stare into the distance, unmoving, seeing nothing, only knowing that somewhere out there is our little girl. I hope, and believe, she is happy.

If you decide to camp at Sakatah Lake State Park, even should you not be staying in the camper cabin and so have no need to go past the parking lot on the road leading to it, I urge you to take the time to check it out. Should you see in that parking lot someone sitting in a chair and staring off into the distance, or, should you just see an empty chair, find another place to set up camp. Too many people have left loved ones behind for another family to add to their number.

# INJUSTICE

## A GLENDALOUGH STATE PARK GHOST STORY

SOMETIMES THE WAY things are, it just isn't right. The guilty don't suffer the consequences of their misdeeds. The innocent pay the price. That's the way it is for those campers who choose to stay in the cabins at Glendalough State Park. The couple who left Brian Axelson to freeze to death at the park entrance never underwent the punishment for their crime such as is prescribed by Minnesota State Law for those who commit murder in the first degree. For the campers it is a different story. Many would prefer serving a prison sentence in the state facility at Stillwater to spending another night in a Glendalough cabin.

Ending a business partnership can be a problem if one of the members of the arrangement is not aware of the considered dissolution and, if so informed, would not agree to its terms. In this particular situation the terms were that Richard Young and Denise Collier would get everything and Brian Axelson would get nothing.

The partnership under consideration involved supplying drugs to meet the needs of Minnesota's addicts. Business had been good. As is sometimes the case when a considerable amount of money has been acquired, the thought arises, Why Share?

On one of the few occasions when Richard and Denise had not been so stoned that no actual thought was anywhere within the realm of possibility, the idea of dissolving their partnership with Brian Axelson occurred to both of them together.

The three—Richard, Denise, and Brian, shared a house in Morris, Minnesota, where Richard and Brian had met while enrolled as students at the university. It had been their mutual drug dependancy that brought them together. It was that same interest in mood-altering substances that created the partnership in which they were engaged.

Brian, who had majored in chemistry, whipped the stuff together in the basement of their rented property. Denise did the shopping for supplies. Dick distributed the finished product. The split of fifty percent for Brian and twenty-five percent each for the double Ds seemed fair enough at the beginning. As time went on, the two Ds wanted a better share. Their goal being one-hundred percent for themselves.

One of the things about operating illegally, as

the threesome were certainly doing, was that the word "cutthroat" used to describe competition in business becomes a verb as well as an adjective. While Brian labored in the basement, Richard was out on the streets. In the basement, Brian faced the possible danger at one of his mixtures reaching an explosive point in its manufacture. That could blow him and the house all to hell. On the street, Richard was experiencing the actual danger of the drug business—unfriendly competition, the desperation of addicts, the threat of arrest. His throat had not yet been cut, but he could sense that razors were being sharpened. It was time, he decided, for him and Denise to take the money, all of it, and run.

Brian's expected objection to carrying out that particular plan had been anticipated, and a program had been created to eliminate whatever interference such objection represented. The idea was for the two of them, Dick and Denise, to get away alive and for Brian to stay behind dead. Since it was best that their relationship not come under scrutiny by government agencies, they determined that Brian would have to die by accident. This decision, which seemed advantageous for them, turned out to be less so for visitors to Glendalough State Park.

The effectiveness of the arrangement for Brian's demise depended on the harshness of the Minnesota winter and the damage its chill would do to the unprotected human body. It being mid-January the cooperation of the seasons was in place. It was winter, and it was cold.

Getting their partner into the elements unprotected was made easier by Brian's being a known drug addict. The combination of drugs and alcohol which would be found in the deceased's frozen body would lead to the conclusion that the body's previous owner made bad decisions. An anticipated winter storm of major dimensions met the final requirement for the planned operation's success.

After the time spent together enjoying each other's company rendered Brian senseless, his partners loaded him into the passenger seat of his '96 Saturn SW2 which Richard drove out to as lonely a country highway as could be found in a part of the state fully ladened with lonely country highways. It is regrettable for cabin renters that the chosen lonely country highway connected to the entrance of Glendalough State Park.

It was at such entrance that Richard Young drove Brian Axelson's Saturn into the ditch, leaving it there and dragging its owner, clad in a jacket much too light for the season, a short distance down the road into the park. It was dark and had already begun to snow. With the winter storm warning and the predicted blizzard conditions, the park was empty. Being midweek, even the cabins equipped with heaters for year-round use were unoccupied, Richard and Denise were confident that these conditions would prevent the abandoned car being found and its owner's body being discovered until long after Brian had apparently given up the ghost in a vain attempt to reach some kind of shelter.

In so far as staging their former partner's accidental death and getting away to live as happily ever after as two dysfunctional human beings could ever expect, Dick and Denise's plan had been a success. What they didn't know, as Denise put their Jeep Wrangler into four-wheel drive and plowed through the drifting snow back to the house in Morris, was that Brian Axelson had not been as ready to give up his ghost as had been expected.

While this situation ended up working to the advantage of his two killers, evidence showing his unsuccessful attempt to get his car out of the ditch and his desperate run for safety, it led to problems in the park into which Brian ran to find help that wasn't there.

Cold-stone sober and frantic with fear, Brian had been able to follow faintly visible tire tracks to the campground parking lot that, unfortunately for him, turned out to be empty. With no one there to provide aid, and being in no shape to return to the highway, Brian was at the point of giving up. Just as he and his ghost were about to part company, Brian's will to live was revived by something he thought he saw a short distance away. It appeared, through the thick haze of snow, to be a cabin.

It was, indeed, a cabin. The park had four of them, two of which had what the stricken man needed most, shelter and heat. What all four of the cabins also had were locks on their doors. Desperate, Brian ran from cabin to cabin, tearing open the porch screens only to pound helplessly on the solid wood and solidly fastened doors preventing his entrance to the shelter within. The only hope Brian had was that a park employee had been remiss in his or her duty and left the lock of one of the cabins unsecured.

No such error in performance had occurred. After tearing the porch of cabin four to pieces in a vain attempt to find discarded matches with which he could light something, anything, afire, Brian Axelson filled the icy air with his final screams and curses and gave up his ghost.

Brian's body, found, unthawed, tagged, and sent to the University of Minnesota Medical School, caused problems only for students who had trouble differentiating a spleen from a pancreas. His ghost was another matter.

As with most ghosts, it resisted being found and sent away. Brian Axelson's ghost took up permanent residence in Glendalough State Park.

Chances are, if you visit the park you will encounter no evidence at all that any ghost is there.
You may hike, fish, canoe, cross-country ski,
simply allow the park's special blending of solitude and beauty work its magic in your soul, you

may even set up camp in one of its twenty-two cart-in or five canoe-in sites, without being aware of Brian Axelson's ghostly presence

Only when you stay in one of the cabins is there a possibility of the night being disturbed by an unwelcome visit of what is left of Brian Axelson. The intrusion begins with a noise just outside the screens of the porch, a light scraping as though claws, or hands stiff with cold, were seeking to gain some sort of purchase on the handle of the porch door.

If you hear such a noise, the best thing to do is move quietly to the inner door of your cabin and check to make sure the lock is fastened. You must do it quietly. On no account turn on any light. Certainly do not open the door. You do not want whatever is outside the cabin to know that there are people inside.

It might just be a raccoon seeking out something eatable left behind when the porch was occupied, or, perhaps, a bear also following its nose. It could also be something else, something far more dangerous even than a hungry bear.

Above all, remain quiet in spite of what you hear. What you will hear is the sound of screens being torn, the pounding of someone, or something, frantically seeking entrance to the cabin's interior. Don't move. Don't go near the door. It is not only cats that curiosity has killed.

The noise will continue until it seems the porch of your cabin is being torn to pieces. You may feel the cabin shaking. Don't be afraid. As long as you remain quiet and still and reveal no evidence that the cabin is occupied, you will not be harmed. Whatever makes the noise will finally go away. In the morning, when sunlight gives you courage to open the door, you will see that nothing at all has been disturbed.

None of this may happen. It all depends on the weather. If it is a warm night, as is often the case at Glendalough in the summer, you should not be disturbed. It is only when you feel a chill in the evening air that you must be sure the cabin door is locked before you turn out the light, and be sure to turn out the light. The cabin must look unoccupied. The ghost of Brian Axelson, still freezing from the night of his death, will continue his frantic search for shelter and warmth from the cold which his former friends condemned him to endure.

If the cabins remain as they did during the storm, cold and empty, Brian's ghost will leave after finding no refuge. If, by some carelessness, a person in one of the cabins makes it known the place is occupied, Brian's ghost will not leave without gaining entrance. Once inside, so driven by the same fear, frenzy and violent hatred as on that night his friends betrayed him, who knows what horrors that ghost will inflict on those he meets.

There is, except for warning them, nothing you can do for campers staying in the other cabins. If the ghost comes and you give him no cause to stay, listen as it pays its visit to the other cabins. The night will end with a scream. It may be Brian's final scream as the cold once again claims him. Or, it might be someone who let him in. If that has happened, the scream you hear may have come from them. Just be thankful it didn't come from you.

It's a shame that the innocent people staying in the cabins at Glendalough State Park have to suffer from what others, namely Richard Young and Denise Collier, have done, but that's the way it is, and that's why this story has been given the name, "Injustice."

# A LAUGH IN THE DARK

## A SOUDAN UNDERGROUND MINE GHOST STORY

I WANT YOU TO HEAR ME LAUGH. I have a great laugh. The rest of me not so much. That's why I spend all my time in the pitch black tunnels of the Soudan Iron Mine. I want people to appreciate what they are hearing when they hear me laugh. I have a feeling they won't appreciate what they see should they chance to view the thing, the me, who laughs. It wasn't always like that. When I was still alive, before Phillip Mills killed me, I was appreciated for the way I looked, not for the sounds I made.

In those days I didn't laugh much. I wonder if I ever laughed at all. People would remark on how I didn't seem to have a sense of humor. It wasn't my fault. Back then nothing ever struck me as funny. It's all different now. Now everything is funny. I'm funny. You're funny. Life is funny. Death, mine, maybe yours, is funny. That's why I laugh so much. That's why I want you to hear me laugh.

When I didn't laugh, when I was still a human being, my lack of a sense of humor wasn't a problem as far as having friends. It might seem like bragging for me to tell you that I was the prettiest girl in my class at school. It was true though. In fact, I have always been the prettiest girl, no matter where I was or who I was with. That's all I needed to have friends, just being that attractive attracted people to me.

You would think the girls in my class would have been jealous because I was more beautiful than any of them could ever hope to be. Maybe they were, but it never stopped them from competing with each other in trying to be my friends. I was like a movie star. I think it made them feel beautiful because they were in my company. Being with me might have improved their feelings. It didn't improve their looks.

As for the boys, I don't have to say why they hung around. Early on I learned that, with my looks, I could get boys to give me anything I wanted. I had fun with that. It's been a game, first with the boys around me, then with men. I would get them to give me what I wanted without my ever giving any of them what I knew they wanted. If you think that was mean of me then, just wait and see how mean I can be now.

Things turned around for me during my first job after graduating from the university. I can't say I earned my degree in Forestry. I made sure that before I enrolled in any class the teacher of that class was a man. I could, and often did, fail every test and still got a passing grade, I knew just how to do it.

Up on the Iron Range, where I lived when I was alive, the economy was in bad shape. There weren't many jobs, not that I had trouble getting one. My interview with the guy at the DNR lasted maybe sixty seconds. After looking at me, all he could do was stammer. The only way I could calm him down was to ask him if the people in the picture on his desk were his wife and kids. Then I got the job. The job I got was at the Soudan Underground Mine State Park. You could say I started at the bottom, that being where I am today, down deep in the bottom of the mine. Come visit and hear me laugh.

I didn't intend to stay underground this long. It was the accident that did it. As you probably know, there is this big science thing here at the mine. People in white coats, including a couple cute guys, study things that come from outer space and are small enough to go all the way down through the solid rock to the place they set up their equipment. My first day on the job, when I was shown the underground laboratory, I was told that nothing in the place was particularly dangerous. I believed that. Don't you. There is a machine there that, if you mess with it will turn you into a ghost.

That's what happened to me. How it happened was that the guy who ran the project tried to get me to spend the night with him in that lab in the bottom of the mine.

The guy, Phillip Mills, is in a state hospital now somewhere in southern Minnesota. From what I hear he isn't able to talk about what happened that night in the lab. All he does, they say, is sit on his bed and laugh. Keep that in mind if you intend to try to get a look at me when you visit the mine.

I knew the guy. I used to flirt with him when I saw him coming to work. It doesn't take much for me to make men like him forget they are married, or, if they can't forget, make them wish they weren't.

I could tell he wished he wasn't married. He started telling me about some equipment he wanted to show me. I had a pretty good idea what it was. Whatever it was, I had no real desire to see it, but, I played along. One day, he called up from the lab and asked me to come down and see his stuff. I said, sure. It had been one of those days when nothing much was going on. The park was all but deserted, and I was bored.

It was late in the afternoon. Most of the lab people were taking the hoist up while I waited to take it down. I'm not sure the guy running the hoist noticed me getting on. He was probably thinking about getting home for supper. Anyway, when he sent the cage down to bring up the rest of the workers, I rode along. When I got off the lift and went into the lab, I saw that the two of us were alone. I didn't really like that, so I turned around and headed back to ring for the lift.

I never made it. The project director grabbed my arm and started telling me how beautiful he thought I was, and how much he enjoyed talking with me every morning when he came to work. It was the same old crap I'd heard a thousand times before. I told him so, but he wouldn't give up. He wanted me to stay. When I said I had to leave before the guy running the hoist went home, he told me not to worry. There was a living space in the back, he said, with a kitchenette and a bed. There was food and wine, he told me. We could spend the night.

If the guy had been good looking, it might have been different. He wasn't. Not even close. Then there was all that scientific stuff. It would be like making out in Dr. Frankenstein's laboratory. The whole thing just put me off. I told him to give it up. If he thought I was going to stay down there with a fat, bald, creep like him, his brain must have been damaged by that stuff from outer space.

He wouldn't listen, and he wouldn't let go of my arm. Who'd he think he was? Men like him needed to be taught a lesson, put in their place. I slapped him, hard. He started to cry. I slapped him again, and he got mad, crazy mad. I had seen that before when I told guys to get lost. They lose control. That's what he did. He lost control. If he would have had a gun he would have shot me. If he hadn't been such a wimp, he would have punched me. What he did was push me. That was when I lost my balance and fell into that machine I was telling you about, the one that turns people into ghosts.

I guess that's what you could call me, a ghost. I don't know what else I could be. I don't have a body anymore. That went up in smoke when it came in contact with the machine that was not supposed to be particularly dangerous.

My body was gone, sucked up by the machine. My body was gone, but I was still there, pretty much where I had been, looking at the guy who had just killed me. He kept standing there for a moment, sort of in shock. Then, looking at me, he began to scream. It wasn't like any kind of scream I had heard before, even in the movies. It was as if his mind couldn't take the strain of what he was seeing when he was looking at me. His eyes were staring, wide open, bulging out. Then he threw his arm across his face, turned around, staggered a few steps and ran for the lift. As the hoist carried him up I heard his screams turn into laughter, frantic, hysterical laughter.

From what they say, that laughter hasn't stopped. That's fine with me. The jerk deserved what he got. He can laugh himself to the grave for all I care.

As for me, I hadn't started laughing yet. That didn't happen until I saw my reflection on the screen of one of the lab's computers. I looked funny. It was like I had been turned inside out. My body was gone. Still, I was left with an appearance, an appearance so grotesquely ugly I let out what I meant to be one long, loud, tortured scream. It came out as a laugh.

My whole life had been built on the way I looked, how pretty I knew I was. What had been on the outside had been so beautiful. Now that outer beauty was gone. I suppose you could say it had been replaced by the uglyness of what had been inside of me. You could say that, but you better not say it when I can hear you.

The longer I looked at my reflection on the computer screen, the more I laughed. The whole things was just so funny. I couldn't help myself. I have been laughing ever since. That's all I do. I don't eat. I don't sleep. All I do is laugh.

I laughed as I left the lab. I laughed as I moved into the darkest place I could find in one of the tunnels of the iron mine. I thought maybe, if I could no longer see anything of myself anymore, I could stop laughing. It hasn't worked that way.

I keep thinking of the look people would have on their faces if they saw me. That keeps me laughing. They would look so funny.

Take that as an invitation. Come and tour the mine. I will be down there laughing. I want you

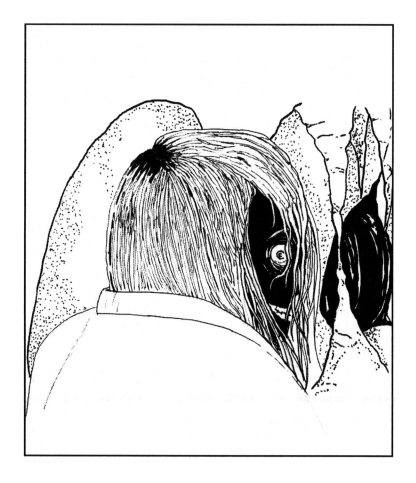

to hear me. You will have to listen carefully. You might have to move away from the tour guide and the group to where it is more quiet. When you do that, I know you'll hear me. When you hear me, I'm sure you will agree, I have a great laugh.

Hearing it, you might want to find out where the laughter is coming from. Go ahead. Although I'm not as pretty as I was, I still want you to see me. Be sure to bring a flashlight so, when you shine it on my face, you will see how funny I look. I bet I can make you laugh.

# FIXING THE BLAME

## A KATHIO STATE PARK GHOST STORY

I T WASN'T MY FAULT. I want you to know that. Sure, a lot of people died. Sure, the Onamia man who lost his wife and four children was convinced it was my fault. Sure, the U.S. Forestry Service determined it was my fault and would have fired me, if I hadn't been already dead. All that may be true, but, I hope, when I tell you my side of the story, you will agree with me that I am not to blame for what happened.

There have been some visitors to Kathio State Park who have heard what I'm going to tell you, but have been too stubborn and bull headed to believe it. I try my best to change their minds. I'm not sure I have ever succeeded. I might have. One or two of them could have changed their minds, just before they died. Don't you worry though, I know you will believe me.

The main reason the whole thing wasn't my fault was that I didn't start the fire. It was two kids from Hillman who were playing with matches. It wasn't until after I was dead that they confessed. It probably wouldn't have made any difference to the Onamia guy or the Forestry Service. The guy from Onamia had fixed the blame for the deaths

of his loved ones on me and that was it. The Forestry Service needed someone to blame. That someone was me. I was the guy who should have reported the fire while there was still time to put it out. I didn't. But, that wasn't my fault.

You don't know what it's like to spend hour after hour, day after day, alone at the top of a fire tower. It is torturously boring. Just to have some excitement, something different in the days that passed by one after the other, always the same, always mind killingly dull, I wanted to start a fire myself.

I didn't though. I never did. That wasn't why I would have been fired or what I was killed for doing. The two kids who did start the fire, and who I ended up taking the blame for, are both dead. I didn't do that either. I would have. If I could have gotten at them, I would have been much more harsh in teaching them a lesson than their parents were. A Mille Lacs County judge put the kids on probation. Kids or not, I would have dragged them to the top the fire tower and tossed them off.

Even though I wasn't to blame, that was what happened to me. The fire was still burning when the guy from Onamia came up the tower steps, crying and cursing and blaming me for not reporting the fire that had killed his family. I tried to explain to him that it wasn't my fault.

I told him I was sick. That's why I failed to report the fire. I was so sick that I had fallen asleep. The report that I was drunk wasn't accurate. The bottle I had brought with me that morning was medicine. I needed it, I told the guy, because I was sick.

He didn't listen. He wouldn't listen. He was like all stubborn, bull-headed people I've been dealing with ever since. When I told him it wasn't my fault, he wouldn't believe me.

I wasn't very strong then, not like I am now. You would be amazed at how being dead builds you up. Now, I could have tossed him off the tower instead of the other way around. I couldn't do that then because I was sick.

It's wrong, just plain wrong to throw a sick person off a fire tower. That's what he did. I was sick, and he threw me off the tower. If you're sick, I won't do that to you. After you listen to me explain that what happened wasn't my fault, and it turns out you are too stubborn and bull headed to believe me, it might help to pretend you are sick when I come to get you to change your mind. I'm not saying that will save you, but whatever I do, I won't throw you off the fire tower. That wouldn't be right.

It doesn't hurt, you will be glad to know. When you hit the ground after falling from the top of a fire tower, it doesn't hurt. I could tell you that it does. That would make you even more sympathetic with the unfairnesss of my situation than, I hope, you already are. It doesn't, though. It doesn't hurt. Remember that I'll be some comfort should you find yourself up in the tower in the middle of the night with my arms pushing you over the side.

What else hitting the ground after falling from a fire tower doesn't do, it doesn't turn you into a ghost. The first time I tossed a person off the tower, I thought it might. I wasn't sure what having another ghost around would be like, especially this particular ghost. The guy I threw off the tower was the Onamia man who killed me. His ghost wouldn't have been good company. Even though it wasn't my fault for what happened, he would blame me and make my being dead miserable for me.

He didn't turn into a ghost, though. Neither have any of the others. It must be that, unlike me, who was blameless when I died, it was their own fault they were killed. They were too stubborn and bull headed to believe in the truth of my innocence. I got to be a ghost so I could convince people like them, and like you, that, being sick like I was, I can't be held responsible for what happened.

It was hard to do that right after the fire. There weren't many people around. For years and years and years, the people who were around just came and went. They didn't stay long enough for me to tell them the story I'm telling you. There were, of course, my Forestry Service replacements in the fire tower, but, after a couple of them accidentally fell off the tower, with a little help from me, they stopped sending replacements. It was too bad for the guys they did send. About what happened, they stuck with the company line instead of sticking with me.

So far, no one has stuck with me. Like I said, on the way down from the top of the tower, before they hit the ground, some might have changed their minds about who to blame for what happened. I don't know that has ever taken place. It's my thinking that if it does happen, if even one person believes that what happened wasn't my fault, I will stop being a ghost.

You could be that person. You could save a lot of lives, your own included, by stopping me from being a ghost. All you have to do is believe that what I'm telling you is the truth. It wasn't my fault that all those people died in the fire, I was sick when it happened. The bottle I had been drinking from was *medicine*.

I thought I had a good chance of that happening, of getting someone to believe me, when the State of Minnesota built this park. So many people would come here to camp. While they were camping I would make sure they listened to my story. Among all those people, hundreds, thousands, surely there would be someone open-minded enough to accept the truth of what I am telling them, what I am telling you.

Even ghosts, though, have their limitations. It takes a long time for me to whisper what I have to say to a person's unconscious mind. Satan could do that in the garden because only two people were there. Sometimes there are hundreds of campers here at Kathio. There is no way I can get to them all.

What I did was work on this guy from Milaca who was writing ghost stories. I got into his head and made him write down my story and include it in his book. I don't know whether he believed it, but he did write it down. That's all I wanted.

This is my story you're reading in his book. Every night I walk through the park, a shadow moving through trees. When I hear people sitting around the campfire telling ghost stories, I stop and listen to hear if they are telling mine. If they are, I wait around to see if there is in that group the one open-minded person willing to believe that what happened wasn't my fault. I have always been disappointed. So far everyone has been so stubborn and bull headed that they have gone to bed unsympathetic and unconcerned about my innocence.

If that's the kind of person you are, stubborn and bull headed, I'll wait until you're asleep. I can fix it so you won't wake up until I have carried you to the top of the fire tower. When I wake you up, I'll give you a chance to change your mind about my story. If you don't do that before I toss you off, you'll have a few seconds to do it before you hit the ground. I hope you will. Then I can stop being a ghost. If you don't, take it from someone who knows, it doesn't hurt when you hit the ground.